The Closets of Heaven

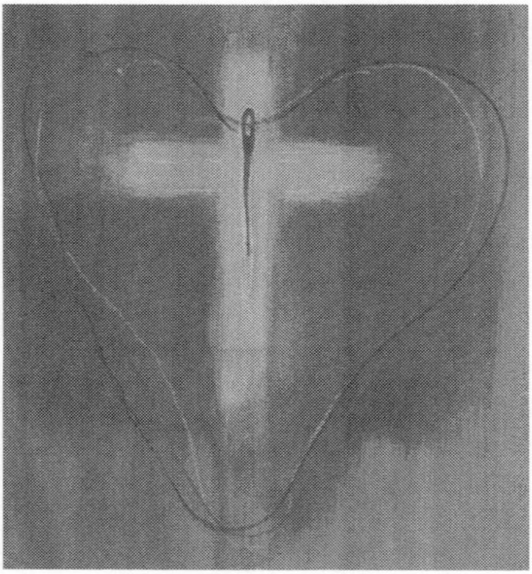

the Closets of Heaven

diane glancy

chax press tucson 1999

ISBN 0-925904-27-9

Chax Press
101 West Sixth St., no. 6
Tucson, Arizona 85701-1000

chax@theriver.com

Now there was at Joppa a disciple named Tabitha, which by interpretation is called Dorcas, or gazelle, who was full of good works and almsdeeds which she did.

And it came to pass, she was sick and died; whom, when they had washed, laid in an upper chamber.

And as Lydda was near to Joppa, and the disciples heard that Peter was there, they sent two men, asking him to come.

They brought him into the upper chamber; and all the widows stood by him weeping, and showing the coats and garments Dorcas made.

But Peter put them all forth, and kneeled down, and prayed; and turning to the body said, Tabitha, arise. And she opened her eyes; and when she saw Peter, she sat up.

And he gave her his hand, and lifted her up; and when he had called the saints and widows, presented her alive.

And it was known throughout Joppa; and many believed in the Lord.

And it came to pass that he stayed many days in Joppa with Simon, a tanner (Acts 9:36-43).

PART I

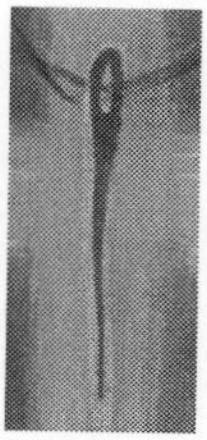

Dorcas's Life

What sort of miracles did he perform, that preacher, he said, turning to the women, and what did he preach about, for that matter?

Par Lagerkvist, *Barabbas*

then airshaft seized, gravity winnowed,

the falling raggedly / reversed, depth

suddenly pursued—

Jorie Graham, *Thinking*

† 15 †

I only want to sew, to have my hands in the threads.

I watch the waves at Joppa stitch the shore. I move my needle like the sea where ships wash to the shore as we are washed into this life. I think we live to do something for someone else. I'm always sewing for others, but it's because I love to feel the needle pull thread through the cloth. Sewing is my prayer. The head is my centurion, not the heart.

The *euangelista* have been to Joppa. They said how Jesus suffered, how he was alone on the cross between the two men. But he kept his head.

I sew my garments with the other women. They come to my house; I listen to their words. We talk about Jesus. We hear that some of his disciples are writing down what he did and said; each one saying it in his own way. There are new scriptures in the making; I want to say, *in the sewing.*

Jesus left upheaval where he walked. There is argument and disagreement everywhere. He called himself the Son of God. He said he was the only way to God, yet our shore is full of gods.

"How did Jesus rise from the dead?"

"Did he rise?" Some ask.

"How can we know what happened?"

Even his believers have different ways of believing which contradict one another. I hear them as I finger the cloth in the marketplace. The shadows of the palm tree move across the rolls of linen as if sewing them.

Jesus was a storm off the sea, a zealot, drifting us apart.

In the marketplace, I hear those who don't believe. They are the Epicureans and Stoics. There is a philosophy for everyone. There is a god for everyone. But all points seem in reaction to Jesus. I hear his name wherever I go.

The women seem the first to believe, yet they speak loudest and most openly. The men don't have to hide what they believe.

The Sadducees and Pharisees argue in the heat.

The Gentiles say they have been adopted by the God of Israel because they believe Jesus was the son of God.

The Jews stop arguing among themselves and set their teeth against them.

The Gentiles are as left out as if they were women.

We hear from Jerusalem that the Christians meet in the catacombs. There are persecutions. There are floggings and other crucifixions. Some of the women cry while we sew. Sometimes we jump at the noise of someone coming, as if we too had to fear. Yet he is the savior, though others say both he and his upheaval will pass.

How do we know what he was?

When the sky is pale, it is a linen tunic. But in the evening, the tunic is wool, draping its blues and reds across the sea.

We hear from Jerusalem that some of the people spoke in tongues in an upper room.

I walk to the fish markets and the street markets where other languages come with their laughter from other places. The city catches the light from across the sea. I walk between the boats and rows of fish and piles of net, and listen to the voices of the fishermen. There is Simon, the *burseus* (tanner), in his oxhide sandals. My sandals are made of palm-bark held on my feet with thongs.

I live in a house with an upper room and a flat roof with stone steps up to it from a dusty street. It is like all the other houses with their perrons. I hear the hooves of a donkey over the few places where there are cobblestones, where they are uneven, uncertain. Sometimes I see the donkeys as little boats on the shore.

I have a pitcher of water at the door I pour over my feet to keep the dust from the sheen of the hard, earthen floor.

Sometimes a child stands at my door.

"Dorcas."

"What do you want?" I ask.

"I want to sew."

The women pray for Joppa as our needles push the shore of the cloth. The landscape is lovely rolling toward the sea. The city is full of good works. The olive orchards shimmer. Everything is as it should be.

The garments we make are *chitones*, *pepla* and *himatia*. They are tunics of different lengths, fastened at the shoulders and tied with a sash around the waist with the fullness at the front and back. Sometimes they're embroidered, brocaded, quilted.

I can't remember the first time I felt the little pain. I think nothing of it. But I feel it. Maybe it is from sitting too long in my chair. I move closer to the light. Sometimes my eyes hurt. My body is stiff.

After the crucifixion Jesus was seen alive. The dead have been raised. The sick have been healed.

For me, it was the way Jesus thought. *We don't live by bread alone*, he said (Matthew 4:4). *But by the act of sewing*, I think he should have said.

After Jesus' death, Judas hanged himself.

A man took the money Judas got for the betrayal of Jesus and bought a field with it.

> *And falling headlong, the man burst, and all his bowels gushed out in the field* (Acts 1:18).

Betrayal has its cost.

So does faith.

We also hear that after Jesus' death, Peter arranged for another disciple, Matthias, to take the place of Judas. Peter is always arranging, always *fishing from the shore.*

I hear the new believers sell their possessions and share things in common. I would not do that.

Sometimes we share our silence as we work.

I see the girl still standing at my door. "I want to sew," she says.

She is like the ocean with a ship on it. A desert with a camel.

I feel sometimes I walk like a camel. The joint on my foot has given away and my large toe crosses over the smaller ones. My foot throbs in my sandals. Both my mother's feet were that way; I remember asking if they hurt.

I get impatient with the women who come to my house to sew. "What do I do now?" they ask.

My needle embroiders the cloth. I don't want to stop. I don't want to decide what they should do. When I sew, my needle is a sparrow taking a dust bath.

I am glad when the women leave. I chase the girl away. I watch the blue sky disappear in its reddest corner. I like my own thoughts. I think sometimes they are an oar.

The man and woman argue again in the next house. I hear them as I light the fire for my olive oil and barley cake in the evening.

I come from two worlds: Greek and Hebrew. I come from two other worlds: faith and works.

I have a house; I am not poor. I sew for others. Whatever is done is done for good. It is done for history.

History is a gazelle; it runs by quickly. It's as though Jesus was just on earth, but now he's gone. It's as if I was a girl and now I'm an old woman. It's as if I was just married and now I'm a widow.

History is an animal. Standing. Running. Sleeping. Killing. Then it is gone. But other histories are born. They are always there.

A gazelle. A history. What is the difference?

By faith I am saved. By faith. That's what they say Peter preaches. But salvation is also by works. That's what I want. When I sew, the power of God is undeniable. I feel my thoughts as I sit in the dark. I have purpose. I have something to do.

Before Christ, I had a ship with only the idea of an ocean. After Christ, sewing is the ocean for me.

I light a torch and walk toward Simon's house, feeling my way along the street, hearing voices from within the houses I pass. In the meeting, they say another apostle, Luke, travels with Peter. In Samaria and Lydda, Luke also was with Jesus, writing about him. I think the disciples have been scattered all over the world. They are dispersed, running from persecution.

When Jesus wanted to wash Peter's feet, Peter asked to be washed all over. I laugh under my breath when I hear this.

Before he died, Jesus told Peter to feed his sheep. That does not make me laugh. Am I a sheep? The daughter of a craftsman. The wife of a merchant. The granddaughter of a woman who talked to me of the ideas men thought.

I think of the sewing while the men talk. Yes, the sewing: embroidery, brocade, quilted work. The tunics, girdles, belts, sashes, cloaks, shawls, mantles. So many worn-out tunics and ragged garments in the marketplace. The children with nothing.

Sewing is the formation of ideas, the thoughts hanging in the *chitones*, the *pepla*. I like the change, the transfiguration of the cloth.

In the street, I hear the crazy woman pass; the one with the cowlick in the front of her hair, making the hair fall over her face.

Maybe she is speaking in tongues.

In Jerusalem, they crucified Jesus on a cross. But *God raised him up the third day, and showed him openly* (Acts 10:40).

I make stitches thinking of our blessings. The olive trees. The orchards. The catacombs that hide the believers. I sew what I see with what I think. I sew garments from the cloth I buy at the wool and linen market. I buy needles too. Some I make from fishbone. I oil my thread.

Clothes are a resurrection.

I try to hold the Christians together with my sewing. I imagine them running. I build prisons for their persecutors with my needle. I stab the persecutors to death with the stitches I take in the cloth. Then I hear about the conversion of one of the persecutors named, Saul. I separate him with my needle. Saul is now a Christian. I know it happens because of the power in the threads.

We are called saints. *Hagioi*. Sanctified by the atoning blood of Christ. But what is atonement? What does it mean to be filled with the Holy Ghost? And what is a soul?

Are we the cloth draped to fit God? Or is he the idea of cloth draped to fit us?

I pray in my thoughts. My words are in the stitches I take with my needle.

One of the widows, who has been sick, dies. I see how thin she is as we wash her body.

"We don't live by bread alone," one of the women says.

I hear the bitterness in her voice.

We wrap the body with grave clothes, winding her feet together and covering her face. She looks like a fish that would feed the *ekklesia* (church) at Joppa. I embroider a pattern to close the grave clothes with my fishbone needle.

We hear from Jerusalem the disciples pray and minister the word. Now the Greeks complain the disciples neglect the widows. But the disciples can't leave the word of God and serve tables.

They call us widows who lodge strangers, wash the saints' feet, relieve the afflicted, were the wife of one husband, are loved by our children. They look at us as though we are pigeons.

> *Wherefore, brethren, look among you for seven men of honest report, full of the Holy Ghost and wisdom, whom you can appoint over this business of widows while we attend to prayer.*
>
> *They chose Stephen, Philip, Prochorus, Nicanor, Timon, Parmenas and Nicolas* (Acts 6:3-5).

But Stephen is stoned to death in Jerusalem and they are down to six. I wonder if Peter will suggest they elect someone to take Stephen's place. If they come to Joppa, I will tell them I can take care of myself.

"And who are the saints whose feet we should wash?" I ask, though I know they are the believers.

At my door, I pour water on the women's feet when they come to sew. "Wipe them on the mat," I say.

The girl wipes her feet twice.

Then Saul, the one killing the Christians and making havoc in the church, is struck by a light on the road to Damascus. He is blinded, and Barnabas leads him into the city by the hand to Ananias, who prays for him. Saul's sight is restored. His name is changed to Paul, and he who persecuted, now preaches Jesus as the Son of God.

The Jews hear Saul, whose name is Paul, and they are incensed. Now Paul knows what it is to run for his life.

One of the women smiles as she listens to the others talk.

I let the girl watch as I sew.

The disciples have to let Paul down over the wall in the basket. He escapes from Damascus and returns to Jerusalem. But in Jerusalem, the Christians are afraid of Paul. They won't believe he is a disciple filled with the Holy Spirit.

The woman talks as she sews. Her threads are artless. The girl sees me watching the woman's needle and she watches too. I nudge the girl's attention back to my sewing. The woman keeps talking. She says that in Jerusalem, Paul gets into trouble again. Now it's the Greeks who want to kill him. But Paul escapes to Caesarea and then Tarsus. Everyone hears about him in the churches in Judea and Galilee and Samaria.

Somehow, the churches keep growing.

Being a Christian is like being threaded through the shuttle that weaves the cloth. I think being filled with the Holy Ghost must be like having your mouth stuffed with threads you try to spit out.

Down in the street there is a commotion. A donkey brays. Maybe he is tethered in the white heat of the sun.

My name means *gazelle*. The gazelle which runs and leaps. I think of this as I sit by the window and sew. Coats and garments, tunics and cloaks. I sew for the widows. Maybe it is foolish; I love to make clothes. Shaping out of shapelessness the cloth that resists. It has to be cut. The cloth has to be sewed. It has to be shaped and held in place by cords and belts. At first, cloth is as unruly as the heart.

What do I understand by sewing? I try to tell them. I am sailing in the cloth. At night I feel the threads around me. That's the way I see heaven: a shaping of the shapeless.

My needle is a gazelle in the linen. How lonely and simple the sameness of each day, unless it is the differences in the clothes I make.

Simon, the tanner, works with his sandals. His house is on the sea. Does anyone question him?

The plainness of the sea has a beauty of its own. I sound like the Stoics I hear in the marketplace. I make a likeness of the sea with my cloth. Forgive me, I say, for loving the cloth, the little threads. I make the garments for others, but it's my own pleasure I get.

I feel the pain more often now.

I think about my husband, my father and grandmother. Sometimes I think they are waiting for me in a corner of the room, by my little table and vial of water. When no one is listening, I tell them to leave. Sometimes I poke them away with my needle. Sometimes I think of Hannah in the scriptures who sewed coats for her son, Samuel. Sometimes I let the girl thread my needle.

Somehow, the food I eat tastes different. I cannot swallow lamb any longer. What will it be like if I die? I hold my tunic closed as I stand on the roof of my house and look across the Mediterranean. I think of Jesus.

> *In the fourth watch of the night, he went walking to them on the sea, and would have passed them by, as if he didn't see them in the wind. But when the disciples saw him, they cried out.* (Mark 6:48-49).

The Christians in Joppa don't have to meet in the catacombs. The meetings of our *ekklesia* are in various houses since the *euangelista* came. The men read from scriptures for hours. For days. They discuss the prophecies while the women listen. They talk about speaking in tongues. Then we take communion and praise our God. Sometimes I feel my fingers move.

Pentecost. What a word. *Pentekostos*, the fiftieth day after Passover. Think of them buzzing with other languages in an upper room. Think of the tongues of fire over their heads. I could embroider them on the pepla. Were they a mirage?

> *It was Peter who told the multitudes that those speaking in tongues were not drunk, seeing it was the third hour of the day.*
>
> *But this is that which was spoken through the prophet Joel:*
>
> *It shall come to pass in the last days, said God, I will pour out my Spirit upon all flesh; and your sons and your daughters shall prophesy, and your young men shall see visions, and your old men shall dream dreams;*
>
> *I will show wonders in heaven above, and signs in the earth beneath: blood, and fire, and vapor of smoke.*
>
> *The sun shall be turned into darkness, and the moon into blood, before the notable day of the Lord come;*
>
> *And it shall come to pass that whosoever shall call on the name of the Lord shall be saved* (Acts 2:15-17, 19-21).

How can Peter speak? The one who denied Christ three times. Maybe God overlooked his weakness. Maybe Peter forgave himself. Does he hear the roosters when they crow? Do they remind him? Is that why he is strong? Because he has so much weakness behind him? Do we live to blunder on? I think God keeps making cloth to cover us.

I let the girl have a needle. She holds it like a wiggling fish, or an eel in a basket, or the worms that come in with the ships.

It was the women who were at the tomb of Jesus first. The little sewing club. They were the ones to tell the men. But it was the men, the *euangelista*, who carried the news on the road from Jerusalem to all of us, that Jesus was not in his tomb.

> *The people asked Peter what they should do now. He told them to repent and be baptized, and they received his words.*
>
> *And they sold their possessions and divided them among all, as anyone had need.*
>
> *They continued daily with one accord in the temple breaking bread from house to house,*
>
> *And the Lord added to the church daily such as should be saved* (Acts 2:37, 45-47).

I know I would not sell my possessions. I would not give my things away. My needles and threads. My bolts of cloths.

The women say what they've heard of Peter as we sew. Peter always must be talking. I hear the women say they wish Peter would come to Joppa.

You can imagine how the Christians upset everyone. No wonder there is persecution of the believers. They want to overturn the old ways with something that goes against the understanding: a death on the cross, a resurrection from the tomb. By faith, we have died with Jesus and are born again. Our self-will is covered with the blood of Jesus. We are now two. Our self and Jesus, who is stronger. So we can draw on him. So we can be made whole in him. Until it seems like we are only him.

Even the believers have difficulty explaining.

The unbelievers ridicule us. I hear them as I buy figs and dates in the market. They are angry at the Christians. They don't like what the men say. They turn away, murmuring.

How many arguments are there? The believers and the unbelievers. The believers among themselves. The unbelievers among themselves. The Pharisees with their talk of angels and resurrection. The Sadducees who don't believe in either. The Stoics, those Job's men, who are fish caught in a net. Who stay there. The Epicureans sorting for their pleasures. The zealots ripping out threads that hold our world.

Joppa is a crossroads for the camel trains and trading ships. It is suspended between land and the sea. I hear the talk of ideas from many places. They blur together like my own heritages.

> *Now Peter was in Lydda and healed Aeneas who had been in bed eight years with the palsy, and he rose immediately. And all who lived in Lydda and Sharon saw him, and turned to the Lord* (Acts 9:32-35).

The travelers also say that Peter has healed a lame man in Jerusalem. The elders and priests and scribes ask him by what power the lame man walks. Peter tells them *it is Jesus whom they crucified, whom God raised from the dead, even by him does this man stand here before you whole.*

The stone which was called unimportant by the builders, is become the head of the corner.

Don't worry about Christianity, Gamaliel says to the unbelievers. *If it isn't true, it comes to nothing* (Acts 5:38).

Joppa is a seaport town. Have I said that? Situated on the Great Sea, the Mediterranean. Little Joppa with its cargo of good works sent out to the world.

Jerusalem is nearly a day's journey on a donkey. I have never been anywhere but Joppa. The ships must look at me strangely when they come to the shore. They must be like camels passing a tree that has to stand in one place.

My name is both languages. Dorcas is Greek. Tabitha, Hebrew.

I could have run a shipyard. I could have been a merchant. But I sew. It is the only voyage I have. I own my house. I am the captain of my own place, yet I am alone. I sit all day and sew. Sometimes my legs tremble when I stand. Sewing has its costs. The pain holds my body with its rope. I think I run like a gazelle toward death. Sometimes I feel my house has sails; I feel I am on the sea. I only have to look out my window to see the waves. Sometimes when I climb the stairs to the roof, I say I am standing on the ship's deck.

The pain is worse. I cannot eat figs any longer. They feel like donkey hooves in my mouth.

There is healing in Christ. I open my mouth. I try to speak in tongues. I hold up my hands. His words are my fish and bread.

Is tongues not a gift the Holy Spirit gives to his believers? If they are good little donkeys. If they carry the burdens they should.

In the meeting of our *ekklesia*, I hear one of the men read:

> *Forty years God sustained them in the wilderness. They lacked nothing. Their clothes did not get old* (Nehemiah 9:21).

"Their clothes did not get old?" I ask suddenly. "Their clothes didn't wear out? What kind of threads made them? Did some angel remake or mend the robes as the people slept? Did God breathe upon the cloth at night? How could cloth not wear out? Just look at the ragged children in the marketplace."

The people look at me. Why don't they say something?

"Cloth wears out," I say.

What did their clothes look like? The skin and bones of them. The texture and movement. How did the robes change from day to day? How could sameness work in cloth? Clothes are supposed to change, age, die. What if they didn't? How did the robes feel? Were the people aware their clothes didn't wear out? Something that didn't change didn't belong to the person who changed as they wore it. I ask them in the meeting, "Why am I the only one who thinks of this?"

Sometimes I can only work a few hours. My body throbs the way my foot does. I think my foot is now my whole body.

I walk to the market for herbs and lentils. I walk on my camel foot.

I want to push the crowds out of my way. The goats and rams. The little crates of chickens. The rooster. Pigeons. The noise of them all. The juggler tries to get my attention. I push him with my basket.

Maybe I'll walk across the water; they say Jesus did. I want to walk across the sea where merchants come from far places. Sometimes I hold to the side of the houses when I return from the market.

Simon, the tanner, carries my basket of fish. Does he think I'll ask him to share it with me?

I hear the language of others on the street. It must be like tongues in the upper room. Everyone speaking their own language; no one understanding, but I know it is serviceable. I know it is language. Not a voice wasted. I do not think the Holy Spirit visits me with tongues.

Who is the Holy Spirit? A *phylax* (guard) who watches a sepulchre? A shadow who won't let me pass?

My voice is in my threads. Sometimes I hear them speak. I think the sound of my sewing has the power of a tongue. I feel the needle in my hand. My hands tremble as I work. I see the women watch my hands. I wonder if they hear my threads.

"I will help you with the needle," the girl says.

"You can't even hold your own needle the way I say," I tell her. "How can you help me?"

She sits beside me on the little foot stool watching her feet when I am angry with her.

Why am I angry?

The threads chap my hands. I rub oil on my fingers. They smell like flax. They are rough as the dried nets of fishermen.

I want to walk the dusty streets of Joppa, but my feet won't walk.

In the night, I think the sea is dry. The ships have wheels like a cart. They are pulled by donkeys and camels.

I think of Noah, or John the Baptist wearing skins, with his hive of bees.

I can't stand on the roof at night and look across the sea. But I know there is something moving over the world. All worldly. I feel a pain sharp as scissors. My mattress is wet with sweat. I shiver in the night breeze. I can't lean down to pull up my covers.

A needle is the rage of heaven. (To sew keeps the fish away.) (The conspiracy of fish.) The fish have legs they open from their side when they come to shore. They walk through Joppa at night. Sometimes they step into the sky.

When the women come to sew, I ask them to move my bed so I can see the sky. I don't tell them the stars are fish in the dark. I don't tell the women how the fish scales glisten in the room. The fish are taking over. They are jugglers in the marketplace. The fish sweat as they try to get their breath.

I dream of a foot with eyes and ears. The women's voices have edges of a sparrow's chirp.

I hear the crazy woman in the street. I think she speaks in a trance.

The women have threads hanging from their eyes when they come to my house. They have fishermen's floats for ears. Sometimes I cannot even sit up in bed. The women prop me against a sack of cloth. I grip the edge of my mattress. My breath won't come.

I feel the scissors again. Someone is cutting me out of my body.

Then there's another pain. Unlike the others. Maybe it's the girl trying to stitch me with her crazed needle.

I see the walls of my room transfigured as cloth. They move closer when they don't think I'm looking.

The sky has a moon and a sun for eyes.

There is a bleeding hand above my bed. It must have been poked with a needle. The blood drops on my head.

Something like the sun from the other.

How much fabric of days and nights?

The women sew in my house. They swim through my room like fish. They nibble my arms. I try to hold my arms away. They hold my arms down so they can eat.

Is that my own voice I hear? It sounds like someone howling.

The moon is a leper's hand without fingers. The moon is the palm of a hand. The shape of the moon is a hand of another shape.

What is that clanging?

Water is squeezed into my mouth from a cloth. Once I choke.

The moon is stabbed. Blood drips from it.

Death is facing the self by itself. The women are with me. But it is myself I sit by. The hard little knot of the self.

My lungs suck for air.

The sun turns cold and goes out with everything in it.

PART II 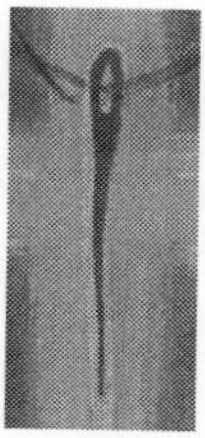

Death

Each of us finds the world of death fitted to himself.

Virgil, *The Aeneid*

Dying is not a dry sea. It is walking into the water. I don't want to get wet. I don't want to be with those who swim and move their gills. Their large eyes. But these aren't fish here, but old beings who walk with me. They are kissing my legs. *Get away*. I poke them with my needle until they are full of holes.

I try to speak, but the soggy shore sinks under my feet. I am going somewhere, but I don't like it. I must think to keep my head. I must remember; must imagine. My needle swings in the cloth. My needle follows Christ. My needle is Christ.

There is a floating, the way fish move one way and the other in the water. There is always a needle bobbing through a cloth. I take faith from my needle. I must not forget to connect. A needle has roots. I feel the body of the needle. The bird of the needle. A needle is a stem from which heaven grows. It is a core; a kernel. It has the smell of the sea. A needle bobs like a boat. I cannot let go. I cannot let myself be pulled away. What is happening? My thoughts are waves running everywhere without a needle stitching them.

The nostrils of the camel widen when they smell the sharp water. A needle draws throats together.

You can cut your foot against the sea. Whole continents overlap the ocean. The thoughts of heaven spill like waves to the shore. I think of a fisherman's float. Nets of fishes. Their eyes embroidered by a needle. The angels sew the scales on the fish. They sweat in the heat. A littler angel wipes their foreheads. Heaven is full of perrons.

> *It is he who builds his stories in the heavens, and has founded his troop on the earth; he who calls for the waters of the sea, and pours them out upon the earth: The Lord is his name (Amos 9:6)*

Heaven is full of thoughts. Just as I wanted it to be. One thought follows another without pausing. I fly on the winds of thought.

The camels turn back toward the desert where they want to go.

The sandstorms are needles traveling to Joppa from the desert.

I think of them on the shore of heaven.

Quiet. Listen to the needles. They talk, but they don't think I hear them. Sometimes I hear them speak in tongues. I don't understand their words, but I hear them. The needle is a wound. It heals by faith. It is a ship that travels where I can't. It is a flock of sheep. A harbor from the sea.

In heaven there is a family of needles: Grandmother. Father. Husband. Children.

The church of needles sticks in the folds of the ocean. There is drying in the needles. They walk to the shore.

I put my hands to my head to feel my thoughts.

The trees are needles in heaven.

I say, *up somewhere*; there: Jerusalem, a city of New Jerusalem.

I learn that I have to learn scriptures to get into heaven. I see there is something I can't see beyond. I see the dead memorizing the words.

> *You clothe yourselves, but there is none warm* (Haggai 1:6).
>
> *Don't be anxious about what you wear. God clothes the grass of the field. Shall he not much more clothe you?* (Matthew 6:30-31).
>
> *I clothe you with a change of a garment* (Zechariah 3:4).
>
> *Have you clothed his (the horse's) neck with thunder?* (Job 39:19).
>
> *The pastures are clothed with flocks.* (Psalm 65:13).

I say my own scriptures. *He clothes the sea with waves.*

God does not like it. I have to get back in line with everything I learned.

There is drying in the scriptures.

I think, in Joppa the women are washing me and draping me in cloth. I can't feel their cloths streaking my arms, but I think they are. Maybe the girl is standing with them.

I want to be with Christ and his saints, all sewing. Even Christ embroiders. Sometimes I see beyond the fog. I see heaven's storeys are full of thread. I see circles of needles in heaven. I never have seen such spirals or such patterns. I could never imagine them. No. Storey upon storey. Place upon place. Heaven upon heaven.

Beyond the scriptures, I see there are closets in heaven. Full of shawls and mantles. Tunics with sashes and belts. I see the tunics becoming ephods. They are also tied with sashes, but held at the shoulders with shining ornaments as if little moons. I see the transformation of cloth. The resurrection of sewing. Plain shawls and tunics become priests' coats and robes, ephods and breastplates, girdles and mitres.

Maybe the river of heaven is for washing the clothes.

I want to say, I am the Bride of Christ. I am the Bride of Heaven. I am the Bride of New Jerusalem.

My husband is here. We are spirits meeting one another with reserved joy. I can't say that I see him clearly; he is in a fog. I would think we were in Joppa those evenings the fog crowds in from the sea and the stars don't flicker. I speak briefly, but after that I can't think of what to say.

I clothe the heavens with blackness (Isaiah 50:3).

It is my grandmother's thoughts I hear. But when I turn to her, she has moved on. I want to sew threads that look like her voice when it left her mouth.

I look for my father.

What else is up here?

Who are they thinking?

This is death?

I will say, I am a widow doing what needed to be done. I will say, when we met for water at the well, I could see the worn folds in their garments. I wanted to sew for them. I wanted to clothe them. I watched them walk from the well with their heavy earthen water-jars. I only thought of them.

I am still in line. There are people ahead of me with their arms missing; parts of their bodies bitten away.

> *...there shall be a resurrection of the dead, both of the just and unjust* (Acts 24:15).
>
> *And many of those who sleep in the dust of the earth shall wake, some to everlasting life, and some to shame and everlasting contempt* (Daniel 12:2).

But which line am I in? Do we stand in the same line to be separated? I look for someone I know. I look for someone to tell me.

God is trying to take the needle from my hand. I will not let go. I can't get along without it. I want to embroider the circles of heaven. *The layers of the heavenlies*. The flying clothes. *Stop it*! I say to God. I jerk the needle away from him. The needle is myself.

I want to step onto the ridges of heaven. I think they are thoughts.

There are closets that move outward in a coil. Blessed needles. Holy ephods and mitres. I am coming.

Tabitha.

I look to see who addresses me by my other name. Who is it? Someone I don't know. Surely.

Death is a relief from suffering.

There is goodness. I could last. As long as there are needles and thread.

Some of the women were in their pleated *chitones*.

I see God and his brooches. The main fullness at the front and back, not bunched at the sides. It is not simple to drape the tunics, the shorter *himatioi* with scallops.

Sometimes I walk by the sea to feel the scallops on the shore under my feet. The sea is a moving garment. A living garment.

I have another scripture verse to learn.

> *When you pray, go into your closet, and shut the door…* (Matthew 6: 6).

What good does praying do now?

There are seams of thought after the world. I stand on the selvedge.

It is like the nights that are full of the moon and I stand on the roof of my house and look at the sea. I know what the sea looks like during the day, but in the darkness, I can only see the shadows of it.

That's where I stand on the shore of heaven. Trying to look ahead.

But I don't go forward as yet. I know what's there. But it does not yet have words.

Someone keeps calling me, pulling me back.

I drive him away with the sword of my needle, but I hear his voice again. *Tabitha.*

There are stories returning the dead.

> *Elisha went up, and lay upon the child, and put his mouth upon his mouth, and his eyes upon his eyes, and his hands upon his hands: and he stretched himself upon the child; and the flesh of the child became warm.*
>
> *And the child sneezed seven times and opened his eyes (II* Kings 4:33-35).
>
> *My daughter is dead; but come and lay your hand upon her, and she will live* (Matthew 9:18).
>
> *They brought the young man (Eutychus) alive, and were not a little comforted* (Acts 20:12).
>
> *Everyone will be raised* (I Corinthians 15:52).

We have the scriptures. We heard Christ's words. We heard what was happening in Jerusalem from those who passed through Joppa.

How much this place is like those words.

Beyond the closets, I see a vast city of people. Streets. A river. Somewhere a throne. I see heaven is full of flying beings. Birds. Crowned pigeons. Their eyes red as heaven. Their breasts blue as the sky and sea at dusk kissing. Their headdresses topped with white-tipped feathers. They have constellations on their heads. There are *granges*. Words I don't know. Palm trees in oasis after oasis. Landscapes of mountains and desert. The elements are in heaven: wind, the draperies of light. Creatures I have not seen wearing tunics with slits or cuts from which light sneezes. Animal beings wearing something like fish scales, something sewn as if it took words to tell. Others have feathers as if vents of the smallest windows. And there's the noises. The singings. Winged gazelles with spots and stripes.

There's a hierarchy in heaven.

Closets of garments I have sewn. I cannot explain.

I wish I had used more than one thread on a needle. Threads of different colors. Why didn't I know? Maybe if I had prayed. Maybe if I had tongues. Why didn't God make it clear? I feel my anger. I want to rework all I have sewed. I see the garments differently now; I see them as garments within garments.

Everything seems sudden. As if forming. The cloth cut but not yet sewn.

What is happening? Everything changes. I feel I am falling. My house, the ship, is sinking. What do they do at sea when their ship is going down?

Those women in my house. Is one of them helping the girl sew?

Back into the soppy water.

Peter is praying to Jesus. Peter is asking him to call me back.

Calling me to this word, this call, *this*.

I feel the tenderness of the cloth over my body. The group of women. They cry and I want to tell them not to cry. Then Peter comes and they plead with him. I am far away when I hear him say; it is simple: *Tabitha*. I open my eyes and see the disciple. I know he is Peter. The power of his word pulls me. I am on the shore of heaven when I hear his voice. I am stepping into the circles of heaven that last forever. I am a captain of the sea of needles. And Peter calls me back! I can't move my feet. They are held together with fins as a fish's. I see the starfish in the water. I see they are my hands. I have become the sea.

Heaven is a garment I wear. The lovely folds of cloth flowing.

But a voice calls me back. It has been done before. Don't I know.

I feel my feet caught in a fish net. I am not finished with seeing yet.

Thruck. I feel the gauze of the world is mesh. The nets *enmesh*.

There are spaces somewhere between the seas in heaven, and a voice that calls me back.

PART III 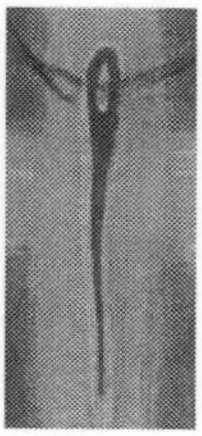

Peter Calls Her Back

....like a broken tooth and a foot out of joint.

Proverbs 25:19

Why would I come back to life?

To hear the leper's bell? To be followed by the crazy woman? To watch the waves of her hair? To see the lame? Blind? Deaf? To live without the circles of heaven I saw? Why would I want to return to this ugliness? Ugliness.

Peter has my hand; I draw it back. I want to snip off his arm, but I remember I must be polite.

There's something strange in my room. Strange. What am I doing here?

"She's alive," Peter says and looks at me like he hardly believes it himself.

I don't seem any different. I don't know what to say. What does he want? We are standing in my room, but I can't take a step because the grave clothes are bound at my feet.

The room is stark. Ugly.

I am hungry for heaven.

Peter calls the women into my room. They stand gawking at me. No one knows what to say. They are amazed I am alive.

Peter leaves the room.

One of the women helps me to sit on the bed. They undo the grave clothes. The girl stands at my side.

"I am thirsty," I say.

The girl brings my pitcher of water.

Someone hands me the tunic they left on a peg, but it is soiled. They didn't have time to wash it, they say.

I ask for the women to leave me alone. I feel if my hair is tied back like it always is. One woman stays to bring me a clean tunic. I ask the girl to leave.

Downstairs, I hear them talking to Peter. The woman helps me dress, then leaves the room also. I sit on the bed. I want to cry, but I will not let the tears run down my face. We don't always get to do what we want, I tell myself. But I am angry. The first time I was going someplace, I was returned to Joppa.

I am bothered by the ugliness for a few days. I can't tell them what I see, but there are lovely clouds over Joppa, like the underside of heaven. And there are ships spinning on the ocean, and sewing, yes, sewing.

At first, the world does not seem to fit. But I sew the city. Whole worlds in my hands.

They look at me when I walk to the fish market on the shore: the women with their bundles and palm-frond baskets. I do not like it. I see the juggler; the traveling players with their puppets. My lungs fill and I want to cry out for the world, for the lost and suffering people, but I sweep the feelings back. The Holy God loves his minnows. He gives us Jesus, the minnow basket. Jesus, the minnow lover.

Will I feel pain again? Will I have strength to sew? How will I die again?

The stars are lanterns in the heavens. The flames waver in the evening breeze from the sea. Someone is stitching by her lamp. I can follow the pattern like birds in the open air.

At night I lift my hand to the sky as though God will pull me back.

I have fits of hunger for heaven. The vast coils that move outward. I see them in the spirals of a tiny shell. I open my mouth and bite the air.

I see we are what we make ourselves to be; in Christ, of course. The heaven I saw was his, his open rooms; closets full of enormity.

Now I walk through the markets in Joppa. Over there, I see Peter by the stalls and booths.

Do I feel the wind from the sea? Was I sucked through the water on my way back? Yes, we get to the earth through the sea. Isn't the birth of a child the arrival of a fish?

The girl follows me through the booths at the market, past the braying animals, the tethered bullock. She stumbles on my tunic as she watches the players with their puppets. She wants me to make a puppet for her.

I watch the players move the puppets. Is that the way Christ works with us?

"Look here," I tell her: The flour of wheat, barley, spelt, millet; olive oil from the stone presses; beans and lentils; the raisins and figs, dates, apricots, pomegranates, almonds, apples, mulberries, melons and lemons; the cucumbers, onions, leeks, garlic and endive. Salt, cinnamon, rue, dill, cumin, coriander, capers, saffron and mustard. Lamb, fish, beef, veal, doves, sparrows. I go over them as if they were stitches I take in my cloth.

Now the girl watches the woman with the grasshoppers. She watches her remove the head, the feet, the wings, the entrails. She watches her take the other grasshoppers that have dried. She crushes them into a cake, and cooks them in water with salt, or fries them in oil and served with honey.

I think about Hannah in heaven. I wonder if she still sews little coats for her son, Samuel. Maybe in heaven (if I had stayed there), we could sew together at her house.

What is a soul? Maybe it is a fish that lives in the sea which heaven is, which is somewhere in the head when I die, when I am clothed with the sea, when I have what I learned on earth.

> *Now there was a certain man of Ramathaim-zophim of Mount Ephraim, and his name was Elkanah.*
>
> *And he had two wives: the name of one was Hannah, and the name of the other, Peninnah. And Peninnah had*

> *children, but Hannah had no children.*
>
> *And Elkanah went out of his city yearly to worship and to sacrifice unto the Lord of hosts in Shiloh.*
>
> *And when the time was that Elkanah offered, he gave to Peninnah, his wife, and to all her sons and daughters, portions.*
>
> *But unto Hannah he gave a worthy portion; for he loved Hannah: but the Lord had shut up her womb* (I Samuel 1:1-5).

When Peninnah taunted Hannah because she was barren, Elkanah, the husband, asked her why she wept. Wasn't he better than ten sons? No, I think of my old husband. I think of the children. No, he wasn't. But Hannah kept praying for a child. She vowed she would give the child to the Lord. She prayed so hard, the priest thought she was drunk.

> *And Hannah bore a son named Samuel saying, Because I have asked it of the Lord* (I Samuel 1:20).

And Hannah took Samuel to Shiloh and left him with the priest. How hard that must have been. But we all lose our children one way or another, though, later, Hannah had other children.

When I walk to the market, I always see Peter. I try to be grateful, feeling awkward with him beaming over me. I was dead and now I live. He touches my shoulder, and I want to withdraw. I don't like going to the market. I don't like everyone looking at me.

Sometimes I look for the flying beings I saw in heaven. The ones with red eyes.

Sometimes I sew several threads together. The way I remember. How can I make the sewing look like what I saw there?

Sometimes when I look up from sewing, the women look away from me quickly.

I blot the tea I spill when I rise quickly to get the door. I'm not used to company. I'm used to being by myself, except for the women who sew. I abide them, but I feel frightened at the arrival of the others. I stand at my door and look. Then they are in my house asking questions. They don't sew, but they want to know what was it like; what I remember of death.

Do we remember our sins? They ask in *ekklesia*. What is it like to see heaven?

I say in heaven I should try not to sew. But I cannot stay away. The needle jumps into my hand. The voice is a needle sewing. What have I forgotten? I say, I think we recite scriptures in heaven, or just before there. I say I remember hearing Hannah's thoughts.

> *The barren have born seven; and she who hath many children languishes.*
>
> *The Lord kills, and makes alive; he brings down to the grave, and brings up* (I Samuel 2:5-6).

But how can they prepare? They ask.

They have to walk into the sea, I say. Not the shore of Joppa.

No. There's another shore. Somewhere.

"But where?" They ask.

I try to sew. But they keep asking. I was there. How can I not talk of it? I run into a storm in my sewing as I talk.

Heaven, or the edge of it, which is all I saw, I tell them, is a crowd on the shore when the fishing boats come in. Everyone hurrying for the fish.

There is confusion. Shoving. Irritation. I think now, none of it was clear. Heaven hides itself. Heaven is clothed. Heaven is closets. Full of marketplaces with multiple happenings. Clefts in the rock. I am not making sense. Weren't there even stalls and closets and storeys in the ark?

I see they are disappointed in what I can tell them.

In the scriptures, there are what seem to be sewing lessons. I think sometimes I want to teach. I want to tell the girl that Hannah's little boy, Samuel, wore coats she made for him. She took them when she went with her husband from Ramathaim-zophim to Shiloh to offer the yearly sacrifice.

When Samuel became a priest, he was clothed in a linen ephod, which is something (being a priest) I tell her she couldn't do, while she's in this life.

I tell the women God cares for sewing. His instructions for the ephod and the holy clothes are in Exodus 28.

It shall have the two shoulder pieces thereof joined at the two edges thereof; and so it shall be joined together.

And his sewing (Aaron, the priest's) shall be heard when he goes into the holy place before the Lord, and when he comes out, that he dies not.

I think I will make ephods, which are tunics before their transformation. I think of cutting the hole for the neck, and sewing the woven work around it. My ephods would fly around the room like birds.

The words about sewing lift from the scriptures. They make their way into my head, onto the shore of my thoughts, into the determination of my will. I think we live to sew.

I seek wool and flax and work with my hands.
I am like the merchants' ships. I bring my work from afar.
My lamp does not go out at night.
I work at my spindle and my hands hold the distaff.
I stretch my hand to the poor.
My household is clothed with scarlet.
(Proverbs 31:13-14, 18-19, 20-21).

I am always high with scriptures. Why? I am still learning verses.

Time is an emptiness. What will I do if I don't sew? I have to have purpose. I have to know what to do. The words about sewing speak to me.

I can't pass a day without knowing I will accomplish something with my efforts. I watch the path of my needle through the cloth. I can forget time; it is timeless, because of the loveliness of sewing.

I wait for another morning in my bed. Sometimes I think I can work by my lamp through the night, but my eyes sting. Sometimes the needle fuzzes as it goes into the cloth. I want to say, *fuzzle*. I decide to turn out my lamp. Lord God of hosts, keep my eyesight. Keep my ships in the night. May I not have been brought back to be blind.

If only linen would hold dye, I would use the purple from sea mollusks and the *tekhelet*.

The girl does not come. We hear from a neighbor there is a disabled ship trying to enter the bay. We leave our sewing.

The *artemon* (the foresail) sticks up like a cross from the water. I see Peter praying. The sailors will not be able to bring the ship into the harbor. Several boats row toward it. The oars are the wings of small insects. We hear the sailors yell as the ship sinks. The divers cannot retrieve the cargo, any of it. The rescue boats are loaded with men as they return. The captain paces the shore when the fishing boat brings him in. He is trying to realize what has happened. He is thinking of the cloth that is lost.

The choppy little waves, quick to touch the shore, are nervous sparrows. The larger waves come from the suck of the ship after it goes down. We step back when we see the waves coming.

The noise of the crowd is *spurted*. There are quick, *abrupted* voices. I must get hold of the *klasma* (scraps). Slow them down. Behind them I hear the mourning doves.

I wake in the night to listen to the sailors in the street. They are drunk with the loss of their ship. They want to dive for the cargo. They argue whether is can be done. Leave it in the bottom of the ocean, I would say to them. What is lost doesn't come back. You can pick it up on your way to heaven.

The next morning, I tell the women how to weave their needle through the cloth. Where does their lack of ideas come from? I could not face my days without sewing. Some are just there to talk. The loneliness is deafening.

I put the girl's work on the bottom when she is gone. I don't want it touching mine, or the others. I want a separate place for it. I would like to say, *let the needle rest in your lap. Let it loose a moment*. I can hear her needle grieve over its path, over its lot, over having to go where it doesn't want to; being guided by someone who doesn't know how to guide, whose thoughts don't encompass; who makes it do something it doesn't want. To do lesser than it is capable of when it has a vision of what it can do: that is its fate in the girl's hand. To go crooked and without satisfaction all its days. Plow, little needle in your field from which nothing grows.

She is *kophos* (dull).

Sometimes my needle gives me trouble. I get it back into line. *Do your duty*, I tell it. *Above all, be wise*.

Sometimes I want to beat the walls. I stomp my feet on the floor. I feel so enclosed in this life, I want to poke holes in myself.

Sometimes I think I remember being born. I remember being put in the garment of this body. I remember the tightness around me. I felt my feet sewn to the bottom of my skin. I would be in this small house all my life. No wonder I bucked like a donkey: I wanted to be loosed— the way I was before I was born. I think we long for it all our lives.

A woman gives money to the church and her husband is angry. I hear them in the next house. He starts to beat her. She runs from the house. He beats her in the street.

I take my needle, sew his fingers closed, sew his arms to his body.

What do I do when something I want to do is wrong as well as right?

If only he could see heaven.

I dream of cloth that will fit like the skin of a gazelle. Not like the course cloth we have. Even the wool has a will of its own. But this cloth I saw in heaven, this cloth, is like skin itself fitting what it comes next to. In heaven God knows how.

I prick my finger. My blood is red. But I see blue in the standing veins in my old hands. How does it change? Like a fine silk fabric changes shades in the light and shadows? Like the ground under the olive tree? The sun and shade on the dirt road? The evening sky when I can withdraw into the house and eat my evening meal and sleep?

All the sky changes as it moves. I know the moon is the palm of a hand which bleeds.

What dreams roar in my head like the turning of the sea in a storm? Maybe it's the groundedness so close to the rocking sea. It is the cradle of a child I do not have. Or grandchildren that keep other women busy.

The head is hard. Not like the heart. No, I won't cut the heart loose from the thread that holds it in the chest. But the head, the thinking; that's what I want. Just thinking the thread through the material, planning the cloak. How the embroidery will cross it like a camel.

Christians. *Christianos*. Those speaking-in-tongues-ones. Those give-away-their-possessions ones. They say it that way. Christian. Belonging to Christ.

A fish is our symbol. Because we're going to the sea.

Jesus walked across the water. If I step into it, I would go down like the ship; I would drown. There is no hope of walking on the water for me.

I don't think there is for them either.

The needle sinks into the cloth when I hold it there. Why would Jesus want to walk on water? Now I know it is to keep from sinking.

There are fish in the thinking.

They say Jesus did such things. He pulled a coin from a fish's mouth (Matthew 17:27). I'm surprised everyone isn't looking in the mouth of every fish he pulls from the sea. But I see the coins here, in the waves that spill onto the shore like bags of silver coins. All the people at the fishmarket on the shore. The marks from high and low tide.

Where is common sense? Where is fish sense?

They would stay in the water if they could. The fish don't come on land looking for us.

Blue blood. Red blood. A difference that can't be explained, unless we are like the sky turning red and blue in the evening, unless the sky leaks out from inside us.

Why do we need Jesus? I think in the meeting of the *ekklesia*.

Jesus stirs up the road, even after his death. The dust doesn't settle once he's passed. He causes the people to argue. The women speak out. The men tell us to be quiet. We pray and Peter and the men talk about scriptures. No one agrees. It brings out the worst in us, yet it causes thought.

I was sitting with my husband as he breathed his last breath. It seemed he just folded up like a marketplace at four. Everyone went home and he was no more.

I saw my husband in heaven. I told him I remembered the cornerstone in our house; the ceremony when it was set. We didn't know what to say beyond that. I think about him and miss him. I think sometimes he would flop back as a fish tries to return to water before it dies. But I've died and now I live. What is the difference?

Sometimes in the night, heaven comes in the light of the moon. Heaven is there in the corner of the room. All of heaven? It only enlarges as you see it. How do I explain? Sometimes I stand on my roof and try to see the tunics flying to heaven.

"What should I do with this thread?" the woman asks.

"Snip it off with your teeth," I tell her. I see the cloth pucker when she sews. "Look here," I say, "think of the Lord while you sew. That will help the needle go straight into the cloth. You have to risk *unloading the ship*." I say one thing to her while thinking another.

The girl is sweeping threads, making mounds of them on the floor.

Jesus walked on the earth for a few years and was crucified. Now you find us scattered and ignorant of what was actually meant by it all. If you look away once, just once, it was over.

What are we supposed to do? Join a group and live in the hills eating locust and honey, wearing camel hair and badger skins? I wouldn't like that.

I hear Peter talking. He sees me coming before I can turn away. The people turn and look. Am I supposed to spill over in gratefulness? What does he expect? What do the people want to see?

Peter had to pray to Jesus. It was Jesus who pushed me back to Joppa.

I only want to get past them and go to the market. I want to buy flour and spices, raisins and melons. I only want to get back to my sewing. I listen to Peter talk. I go when I can.

We are in *ekklesia* at Simon's, the tanner's, house. The whole place smells like hide. I don't like to sit without a needle in my hand; I feel enclosed. I make long journeys across the cloth when I sew.

Peter says, "We are saved by faith."

What does he mean? "Can I sit in my house and do nothing?" I ask.

Does he mean, *I can't trust my sewing*? As if it were not a ladder to heaven, as if it were not the wings I fly on. Or the ship I sail upon the sea.

The Christians look at me. There is argument over salvation: whether it is by faith or works. The small group is in an uproar. I sit on one of Simon's stools quivering. What is it I feel? Rage?

When light is on the sea, I watch the needles sewing the water, holding it in place.

I hear Peter talking to the woman whose husband beat her. He tells her to stay with the man. I hear him on the street. Heaven is obedience to God. I do not think so. Who has been to heaven already? Is it him?

I think heaven is far out in the water. The little waves stop, and there is a hole and we sink into it, and become fish, and are caught in the net and suffocate. Then we are scattered into another place.

I divide my days like God.

The Lord God made coats of skins and clothed them (Genesis 3:21). Adam and Eve were dressed in blood. That's what was shed to get the animal skins.

I see Simon and his sandals made of hides. I still wear palm bark on my feet.

Simon in his apron with his vat of salts for tanning. What does he talk about with Peter?

How can I remember what happened in heaven?

Sewing is the way, the truth, the life.

> *Why do you stand gazing up into heaven? In the same manner as he went, he shall return* (Acts 1:11).

Now get busy; work. Weren't those the angel's words?

We are on earth in our skulls with ears and eyes. We wear our veils and head coverings, not knowing anything, not seeing with our stupid feelings, raging and leading the wrong way. No, it is the mind which is the compass, the guide and rudder that says walk on, don't ask, don't know, just live by faith and work.

Heaven is always coming into the room. I think instead they should look into the sea.

Would Joppa float underwater? Would the camels and beavers and donkeys swim if the sea came upon us? Somehow we rise.

They ask me but I cannot say how.

I think the net of stars is our catch. I belong to the fishermen of the heavens. Not underwater.

What gracious God would leave us to rest under piles of water? He promises dry ground. Did not Israel cross?

"Dorcas," the child calls.

"What?"

"Can I come in?"

I don't answer.

"Who are you talking to?" She asks.

"What do you want?" I answer.

"Something to sew."

"You just want to make a mess. I'm busy. Go to the well and fill the jug with water. I want to wash my eyes. They hurt when I work. My eyes feel swollen bigger than a camel's. I think it's the dust from the street. Then you can recite to me. Something they teach you in church."

"But I want to sew."

"Get the water."

There is writing on tablets or parchments the priests can read, but the women have to listen to the priests, or Peter, or the teachers who are men.

What should I do with my thoughts that are always pushing in? I am so impatient. So abrupt. I try to calm myself. I feel my thoughts like garlic and leeks when I stand in the market and turn them in my hands. I also can turn my thoughts over with my threads.

I talk to the girl when she returns.

After the flood, in the scriptures, when Noah and his family departed from the ark on Mount Ararat, Japhet, Noah's son, settled on a hill overlooking a bay. He called it *Yafo*, lovely. Later, Joppa was a part of the allotment of Dan when the tribes of Israel entered the promised land. Joppa on the plain of Sharon. A seaport of Jerusalem.

The girl has to listen if she wants to sew. I tell her, "they wrap our feet together when we die. We walk with what we know." It's why we live. To speak with our threads; our thoughts spilling waves hard as rocks.

"Have you received the Holy Spirit since you believed?" A woman asks as we sew.

"No, but I've received threads," I say.

She looks at me. The other women watch us.

"The threads flow through my fingers," I tell her. "They talk with their tongues."

When we are alone, I rub oil on my sore hands. I speak to the girl again.

> *And the seventh lot came out for the tribe of the children of Dan according to their families.*
>
> *And the border of the children of Dan went out too little for them; therefore they fought against Leshem, and took it...* (Joshua 19:40, 47).

The girl holds her fingers in her ears. I tell her to take her hands away or I will poke her hands with my needle.

I tell her our ears are holes opened with needles. Our hearing comes from suffering. The more we suffer, the more we hear.

The girl says I am mean as her mother. She cries and I take away her needle. I tell her she must think and not cry.

My mother lived by her feelings. I do not want to remember her. I tell the girl if she is quiet, I will give back her needle. We must be quiet and not get in trouble.

I don't want to be a mother angry with her daughter, but the girl is irritating. God must understand. And forgive. The girl gets in the way. She is insistent. She reminds me of when I was a girl. I don't want to remember; I want to leave my anger. I continue talking to the girl about Joppa in the scriptures. Joppa the lovely. If she doesn't listen I send her away. She has to know it.

"Why?" she says.

Because history is a gazelle always with us. When Solomon was making plans to build a house for the Lord, and a house for his own kingdom, he talked with the planners who said,

> *we will cut wood out of Lebanon, as much as you need; and we will bring it to you in floats by sea to Joppa, and you'll have to carry it up to Jerusalem* (II Chronicles 2:16).

Sometimes, just after I returned to the earth from death, I could hear the shouts as they brought the trees to shore. I could hear them drag the trees to Jerusalem.

I think all of history trails behind us in a net.

I read her another scripture:

> *Jonah went to Joppa to find a ship to Tarshish instead of Ninevah* (Jonah 1:3).

"So ends the scripture geography lesson for the afternoon," I tell the girl.

She hands me the cloth she has been working on.

"What happened?" I see the child's arm is bruised.

She got in the way of her mother, she says.

History is a place that heals us, I tell her.

There are old stories of Joppa. Once it was walled. In the fifteenth century before Christ, Pharaoh Thutmose III and an

Egyptian general named, Thoth, put 200 soldiers in baskets which 500 men carried. Thoth feigned surrender. *The baskets are filled with booty*, he said. The gates of Joppa were opened.

The history of Joppa is old. Later, it had fallen to the Philistines, but the people prayed. In the second century before Christ, Simon, not the tanner, of course, but another one, wrestled it from the Syrians and annexed it to Judea.

Joppa is a rolling, rocky place. Our shallow bay is full of rocks which have fallen into the water through erosion from the hill.

When we think of Joppa we do not feel pain, I tell the girl. When we are Christians, the hurt is kept away.

I stand on the roof of my house at night and see the oil lamp burning at Simon's, the tanner's. He and Peter are sharing their thoughts. Why don't they ask me to talk with them? Who do I have to talk to? The women who listen to nothing as they sew. I look to the sky and say, *grandmother*. My father's mother.

Maybe in heaven the clothes are given mouths.

What if all my sewing is waiting beyond what I had time to see when I was there. Or on the edge of there. Clothes that never wear out.

I am sewing closets for heaven where flying ephods land; I worship with my sewing.

Sometimes I see Peter talking to groups of men. The Hellenists. The zealots. The shadow of the palm tree across Peter's striped tunic is like marks of waves in the sand. When I look at him, the sun fades everything in its light.

Sometimes, when I see Peter talking in the street, I go another way. If I see him walking, I step into a doorway until he passes.

Now it is the Gnostics I hear spouting. They would take away the garments the women sew. They dismiss our work as not counting for any spiritual good. Well, give them needles when they stand in line for heaven. Let them sew garments until they hear the threads speaking from their hands.

Now it is the commotion in the street that keeps Peter from seeing me. The sail-makers are carrying a sail to the ship in the harbor. The donkeys bray, protesting the weight. Everyone watches.

The crazy woman speaks like the donkeys.

The women are waiting for me when I return. Can't they sew without me? Am I the only one who has a house? Do they think I'd miss their talk?

What is heaven like? A few of them still ask.

But the closer I get, the less I can say.

Part IV

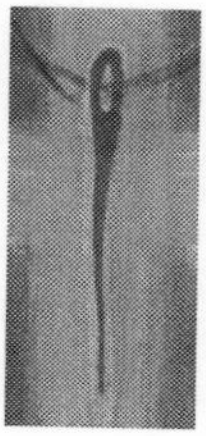

Life after the Resurrection

...the fibre which Clotho packs the distaff for each one...

Canto XXI, *Purgatorio*

Dante Alighieri, *The Divine Comedy*

When Peter is called away from Joppa, some of the men go with him. I watch him from the roof of my house. I do not think he looks up.

Peter walks as if he is a stone, kicked from the hoof of a donkey. Or he walks as if he were the dust the wind swirls in the street, and then is gone.

> *... four days ago I was fasting and at the ninth hour, I prayed in my house, and, behold, a man stood before me in bright clothing,*
>
> *And said, Cornelius, your prayer was heard and your alms are remembered in the sight of God.*
>
> *Send, therefore, to Joppa, and call here Simon, whose surname is Peter; he is lodged in a house of Simon, a tanner, by the sea; who, when he comes will speak to you* (Acts 10:30-32).

"We must sew well," I tell the girl, looking at her crooked stitches. "An angel in heaven may wear what we sew."

I would like to have asked Cornelius what the angel wore.

I'm sure the Holy Spirit filled them with his tongues in Caesarea. I'm sure they run like gazelles on the plain.

The first fifty garments I make go to others. If I need needles, I give them away, then sit in the sun flooding from my window. I wait in faith for more needles to come. Sometimes I see them float in through the light.

The girl waits until I am at a difficult place in my sewing to bother me. "Dorcas."

"What?"

"Can I come back in?"

"Take the bundle of fish bones to the dump."

"Then can I sew?"

"After I rest."

Do we ever leave anyplace we've been?

I watch a spider on the ceiling of my room crossing the surface of the water into heaven.

I think the people still talk when I pass.

Sometimes I remember my sickness. I look at the lamb and beef hanging in the market. I remember thinking, how can I eat? But I think about the scriptures as I swallow.

Once during a famine, Elisha's prophets found some wild vines and gourds in a field, and sliced them into a stew. When they ate, they knew they were poisoned. But Elisha healed the prophets, and the stew, and they kept eating (II Kings 4:38-41).

Could I heal the cloth? The garments?

I can eat. I can clothe.

Thinking is sewing.

Sometimes when I hear the words of the scriptures I feel like I am sewing. Somewhere in my head. The thoughts stitch themselves into the ear. The mind cuts them loose (to wear). They become the *chitones, the pepla and himatioi* of the mind.

Have I said I am Hebrew and Gentile? The Gentile part is divided between those of faith and works.

I walk by the fish markets on the shore. I could step into the sea. I could sink like an underwater ship. I would frighten the fish.

Sometimes I don't eat. There is another kind of food. It comes through the thought. I think in the past, it has come in a time of famine. I am here on earth. I have arrived like a ship from afar. How dare Peter bring me back? How dare the other widows ask him to call me? I was in heaven. I was lifted out of Joppa as a bird. No, as a ship that could fly. Up through the clouds and through the sea on the other side of the sky. I was about to see the mysteries of the heavens. They were stepping out of the shadows, or maybe I was stepping out of the shadow world to them, after I got past my memorizing lessons.

Now I'm back in the dusty, lovely place: Joppa. Where Jonah sailed. Where Hiram of Tyre floated the cedars of Lebanon on their way to Jerusalem, to make Solomon's house and a house for the Lord.

Why couldn't they leave me alone? I was pulled back to a room where a man said, *arise*. He didn't even use my common name, Dorcas. Why didn't he bring someone else back, if he had to bring someone? Why not my husband? My little children? The man with a family? Someone who has something to do? A woman with small children?

What do I do now? Tolerate these women? Wait for another death?

How long am I here for now?

Why didn't they just meet in my house? Speak in memory of me. Did they have to send for Peter? Whose idea was it? Do I have to be here in person? I have the knowledge of heaven with no one to whom I can speak. I have a language they can't understand. I still can't speak in tongues. I am more shut up than I was before. Don't they think about what they did? My needle does. I hear it more than ever now.

My foot still hurts. My camel-hoof foot. My toe could have been straightened. If God could raise me from the dead when Peter called my name, why can't my toe stop throbbing? My foot is a fisherman's boat that can't cross the sea. Was my toe crooked in heaven? Will it be straightened there? I was only there a short time. I didn't notice. But I don't think so.

Sometimes I remember the pain as if swallowing a needle. Sometimes I think my thoughts turn against me. I was there. I am here.

There was a sea of people and beings praising God. Their voices were waves. Heaven was noisy. There was sailing as though a ship arrived each day. Or logs on a float. Somehow, we should worship God. There were markets and wares and hawkers. I think there were magicians and traveling players. I think there were church meetings. I heard the different tongues of language I hear in Joppa. There were ladders and stone steps going up to another roof, and another roof, and up to a multitude of roofs, like the waves I see stretching across the sea, and knew they went on and on beyond which I could imagine.

When they ask me, I say heaven was not one place, but many; but that doesn't say what I saw, but only something like it.

I tell them, "There are the last chapters of Ezekiel. The strange temple there. The closets. The storeys."

The memory of it is going farther away. *Don't go*, I say to heaven.

God is good; there is his goodness here. I must be satisfied where I am.

I look at my chairs and table with a cruise of oil upon it. I look at my blanket and sewing closet, (which I tell God was a dry, covered room where I stored flour, when I still had meals to prepare for my family.)

My house is his. I give it to God; we share it in common. I tell him to come into my (his) house. To sit by my (his) *oikas* (hearth).

My needle is a gazelle through the cloth.

Peter annoyed me when he was in Joppa, but it was the way Christ thought that I like.

> *Jesus stooped down and wrote on the ground with his finger as though he didn't hear them.*
>
> *So when they continued asking him about the woman, he lifted himself up, and said to them, He that is without sin among you, let him cast the first stone at her* (John 8:6-7).

Just imagine.

My fingers are needles. Sewing is my atonement; my savior. My soul is a thought caught in the thinking. I would stand in the open on the roof of my house and not leave, but for the sun, the rain, the night air.

I embroider palmettes, rosettes. The girl embroiders with me. Sometimes I talk to her.

God clothes the grass (Luke 12:28), the girl says. "Why doesn't he clothe his children?"

I look at her. "How can you say such things? Why do you question God? Look at those stitches. The mounds of threads you leave scattered on the floor. What can you do?"

"Who do you think cried for you to come back?" she says to me.

My needle runs aground on my cloth. "What?"

She draws away from me. "I asked for you back. The women sent for Peter."

"Why did you do that?" I stick her with my needle.

She screeches. "They showed him the clothes you made."

This mystery life is. This needle through it.

I make myself memorize more scripture. I buy more oil and sit by the lamp. I make the girl memorize too. She recites to me. I do not look at the tears on her face.

Think of Joseph's coat, I say, a tunic Jacob sewed for his son. Maybe it was like the bow after a rain, with red and the purple *tekhelet* from the sea mollusk, or a shadow of the sun on the sea, or the way a flame sometimes burns in a lamp; the way I feel different shades sometimes when I pull the thread through my fingers. Maybe Joseph's tunic was a shadow of heaven; transparent. You can see through heaven.

In heaven, words speak red and blue.

On earth, I sew sacks and pouches to stuff my feelings into.

> *Think how God clothes us with salvation. Think how he clothes the lilies* (Luke 12:27).

We walk to the hill and watch the camel train arrive at Joppa. They are travelers coming in from the desert. They have walked a long way. I feel the momentum of their journey. Sometimes I think the camels don't want to stop. They could keep going across the sea if the men would let them. They stand in the marketplace where everyone watches. They have carried their burdens. The rodents and vermin scurry. The pigeons and mourning doves fly. *Look at what they have done*, I say to the girl. Just look.

The camels know we watch them. We can see the desert still on them like a cloak. They don't want to sit as yet. They stand with their loads. The men try to get them to kneel. The camels protest. The men let them stand a while longer until the march across the desert fades, until they feel the stopping under their feet.

The girl and I listen to the merchants who have crossed the desert. We listen to the sailors who will take their goods across the sea. Even the camels say what they think.

The men argue about their ideas. The Stoics and Epicureans. But it is their feelings that show.

We watch the magicians in the marketplace.

The piles of goatskins for the tent-makers.

God is no respecter of persons (Acts 10:34), Peter said when Cornelius sent for him. Maybe that's why he allows the girl to come into my house though I pray against her. I put needles in her path. It is because I like to tell her what I think; it is because I have to do what God wants.

Be clothed with humility (I Peter 5:5).

He has clothed me with the garments of salvation (Isaiah 61: 10).

What is salvation? I have to get hold of my thoughts.

As for the madman, *Jesus clothed him in his right mind* (Mark 5:15).

Why didn't Peter heal the crazy woman who stammers, with her hair hanging in her face? Why didn't he heal the lepers? The blind? The crippled? The toothless? The ugly?

Peter is gone; the one who brought me back to life. It is hard to think he is not here. What if I need him again?

We begin to hear about Saul, the persecutor of the Christians who was converted to Christianity. The men talk about him in the meetings of our *ekklesia*. I listen to their voices. Saul is now Paul. He-who-has-two-names goes many places. He is in Paphos, Perga, Pesidia; in the synagogues and churches.

At my house, the women talk about what we heard in *ekklesia*.

Paul is hearing the Jews argue with the believers. He is hearing the Jews, who are believers, say that the Gentiles have to become Jews before they can be Christians.

You have to be born a Jew, a woman says as we sew.

"You can be circumcised and be a Jew," I say. "What's the difference?"

The woman looks at me, but doesn't answer.

I think sometimes Jesus is clothed with the moon; or when it is full, it is a bright window he has opened to look at us.

I do not like scriptures. There's a lot of tearing off and renting of clothes: David, Mordecai, Hezekiah, the prophets and priests. Was there one of them who didn't tear up their clothes?

When Paul and Barnabas were in Lystra,

> *...the people called Barnabas, Jupiter, and Paul, Mercurius, because he was the chief speaker,*
>
> *...and Paul and Barnabas tore off their clothes, and ran among the people crying out, we are men like you* (Acts 14:12, 14-15).

Then Paul went to: Troas. Samothene.

Neapollis. Philippi.

Berea. Miletus.

Ephesus. Perga.

Attalia. Phenice.

Samaria. Mysia.

Bithynia. None of them on the sea. None lovely as Joppa.

What would all that traveling be like? What would it be like to flee? What does it mean that the Christian faith is built on moving? How would they like to sit in their house all day and sew?

The birds are chattering in the palm branches. There is a storm somewhere at sea; I feel the wind tugging it to shore. I tell the girl to stay with me. Maybe I should say, there is a sermon at sea. What funny little seaworms the scriptures are. I feel them coiling in my depths. They are solid as the cornerstone we set for the house.

The storm washes onto land by afternoon. It is more severe than I thought. I think of Simon, the tanner, who lives by the water. The path from God unto our city is wide as the sea. The girl and I embroider a gate to the sea. When the wind blows upon us, it is the girl's cloth that saves us. I see that now. God chooses the lowly things sometimes to teach us.

In my fear, I feel my mother swimming through the house in the storm. I cannot hold on. I put my face into the cloth. I could run faster than my mother on her crooked feet, until she caught me. I thrash as if I had branches of the palm tree on my head. Why couldn't my father stop her? He always was busy with his work.

The girl sews while I cry. My feelings spill from the sacks and pouches I have made for them. I fear the cargo of feeling. It will not sink, no matter how hard I try to push it under the water. Will I have more scriptures to learn? When I am in line getting ready for everything I learned? Will he listen to me? I hear a language in my mouth I had not heard. Sympathy for the girl.

After the storm, we walk though the soggy marketplace. We help the merchants pick up their wares. The meats and spices. Ruined. The grasshopper boxes. One crate with a dead chicken.

Would Peter have spoken the storm away? Rebuked it? Would the storm have listened? And obeyed?

The Stoics say the storm is something we have to bear. The Jews, who do not believe Jesus was the Son of God, say the storm is like the Gentiles who think they are grafted onto the vine of their God. The Hellenists speak of the storm in terms of a war among their Greek gods. The Christians try to explain the loss, but cannot.

We see the mess at Simon's house. His hides everywhere in a heap.

I see designs in the turmoil. I see patterns in the quiet that follows.

Simon tells us the crazy woman drowned in the storm. He found her on the shore by his house. I ask the men to carry her to my house.

The women wash her torn body. I push the hair back from her face and bind it with a thread, then embroider a few threads like storm clouds on her linen cloth. I see the sky is a cloth brought from far away.

The women cover her with spices and I close the seam with patterns of the quiet waves that follow the storm.

I stand at the crazy woman's tomb. I tell her to stay in line. Jesus will answer for her.

"But what if she wasn't saved?" The women ask. "What if the demons had her already, and won't let her go?"

There are some things that thoughts don't answer, but they are still more serviceable than the feelings.

Herod hates the *ekklesia*. We hear he kills the disciple, James, the brother of John, in Jerusalem.

"Peter?" Simon asks anxiously.

We hear that Peter is still alive in prison. Herod intends after Passover to kill him in front of the people. We pray for him in Joppa.

This blood religion. Yes, we are clothed in blood.

Then Simon, the tanner, tells us that Peter is out of prison. He says Peter was sleeping between two soldiers bound with chains, with guards at the door. He heard an angel say, *Peter, arise*. And his chains fell off his hands.

"*Arise*— that's what he said to me in the upper room of my house when he called my name," I say.

"The angel told him to get dressed and put on his sandals— maybe the sandals I made for him," Simon says, " —and Peter followed the angel past the first and second guard, and when they came to the iron gate that leads to the city, the gate opened by itself."

Simon talks so fast I can hardly follow.

"When Peter got to the street, the angel was gone. Peter went to the house of Mary, the mother of John, where they were having a prayer meeting for him. Peter knocked at the door. A girl, Rhoda, came, but when she knew Peter's voice, she didn't open the door, but ran in and told them Peter was at the door. They said, *no, it was his angel.* And Peter kept knocking, and finally they opened the door and let him in."

"Slow down, Simon," I say.

"Will Peter come here?" the girl asks.

Simon recovers his breath. "No," he answers. "He is traveling from Judea to Caesarea."

How do we sew what God is?

In the marketplace, we see the traveling players again.

At my house, we make a puppet for the girl. A likeness of herself: two legs, two arms. We could make the puppet an *euangelista*, I say. The girl laughs. We sew the puppet some teeth. But the girl wants me to use blue threads. We argue. I resew.

The teeth are uneven because I am impatient, and they are blue as the afternoon sea.

On the shore we look at shells. "We will use this pattern for the puppet's ears," I say. "If it is all right with you."

The girl looks at the shells. "The nose?" She asks, holding a long shell for me to see.

"Nobody needs a nose," I tell her. "Just leave the mouth open and air can get in."

She laughs again. We walk on the shore where we see tiny holes that bubble when the little waves retreat. "Eyes?" she asks.

"Yes, them. When I was dead I saw eyes in heaven." Sometimes the memory of heaven comes back like the small stitches I take in the cloth.

The eyes are everywhere, like little mounds of threads with holes in them— with caves in them.

"Everything gets into God's eyes," I tell the girl.

She shakes her head that she knows.

"God is full of eyes," I say again. He has no need of nostrils. But our eyes are dark ships with their cargo-holds where we put cloth.

The girl wants to name the puppet. I say it should not have a name. The girl disagrees. Or we'll call her Hannah, I say, or a name I haven't thought of yet. The girl calls the puppet a silly name, Hannaput.

"No, only I can name it," I say. "All right, then, a puppet with two names. It has two legs, two arms, two thumbs on its fingerless hands, two eyes, two ears. Why not two names?"

"Should we make two mouths?"

"No, only one."

"There are two holes in our nose," the girl says, with her fingers in her nose.

I do not like to argue with her.

Now the girl sits with her hands in her lap. "Make it with a toe like yours," she says.

There are little closets in our head where we keep things. One head is enough. There is a little mouth that says things. One mouth is enough.

Later I sew a tiny shell into the head for thoughts; a shell that coils like heaven which must be in Jesus' head.

We name the puppet Hannaput, the daughter of Hannah.

The daughter of Mary.

The daughter of Elizabeth.

The daughter of Ruth.

The daughter of Leah.

The daughter of Joanna.

The daughter of Rachel.

The daughter of Naomi.

The daughter of Sarah.

The daughter of Priscilla.

The daughter of Lydia.

The daughter of Deborah.

The daughter of Timothy's mother.

The daughter of Jael.

The daughter of Abishag.

The daughter of Phoebe.

The daughter of Rahab.

The daughter of Martha.

The daughter of Jezebel.

The daughter of Rebekah.

The daughter of Susanna.

The daughter of Anna.

The daughter of Dinah.

The daughter of Esther.

The daughter of the nameless women.

All daughters of Eve.

When the puppet dies, we lay it on the table and wrap it in cloth. The girl is the apostle who raises the puppet from the dead.

"What is it like to come back from the dead?" I ask the puppet over and over.

The girl sends her voice into a corner of the room, but the puppet's teeth are shut like the old gates of Joppa. I have pulled the threads too tight.

The girl cannot pound open the mouth, that ship from far away with its cargo in its belly. The girl plays with the puppet more than she sews.

I say, "I have to put the puppet under the grinding stone when the miller isn't looking."

"No, no," the child screams.

But I insist. We have to lose what we are, I tell her.

The girl begs, but I do not listen.

The donkey pulls the stone across the puppet.

The girl will not speak to me.

We embroider.

We walk along the sea. We see the merchants who come to Joppa from the desert; we see the captains who come to land from the sea. We copy the patterns of palm fronds; we copy the light in the water that is pulled from the well.

The *euangelista* who run from persecution stay with Simon and the others before they leave on the trading ships. They bring us news.

In *ekklesia*, we hear that Saul whose name is Paul went to Jerusalem to see Peter. But later, when Peter went to Antioch, we hear they did not get along. Peter would eat with the Gentiles, but when the Jews came, Peter withdrew and would not eat with them.

I see Simon has cleaned the mud from his house. I see how much he has lost after the flood.

"*How can you not be consistent?* Paul asked Peter."

We hear it was no small argument.

"If Peter thought he was justified by faith, why was he relying on works?" Someone asks.

"Because we have to work," I say. What else is there to do? It is the fulfillment of belief.

Why was Peter unclear as to what to do? What was the matter with him? Didn't he have a vision?

> *I was in the city of Joppa praying (this is Peter talking); and in a trance I saw a vision, a certain vessel descending, as it had been a great sheet (or a sail, a mast,) let down from heaven by four corners, and it came even to me;*
>
> *Upon which, when I looked, I saw four-footed animals of the earth, and wild beasts, and creeping things, and birds of the air.*
>
> *And I heard a voice saying, Arise, Peter; slay and eat.*
>
> *Of course I said, No, Lord; for nothing common or unclean has at any time entered my mouth.*
>
> *But the voice answered me again from heaven, What God has cleaned, don't call uncommon.*
>
> *And this was done three times; and all were drawn up again to heaven* (Acts 11:5-10).

My needle is my consecration. Just give me a few threads. There is a holiness so bright in the sewing. Only sewing reaches the kingdom of heaven.

A word leaving the mouth is a thread pulled through the cloth.

Sewing is the flame from the oil lamp. The night *wools* on my bed.

Kurios (Lord), I call, sewing his hands to the sky. Sometimes I want him to take me back; I want my gazelle feet. Then I feel panic because Peter is gone.

Savior of sewing. Savior of light.

I watch the sailors unload an *othone* (sheet of linen).

Be careful, I think.

I see the patterns I will sew along the seams of the tunics. I see the islands and countries between them. A flock of starlings circling over.

Why do we live? To think of ideas of why we live. The thoughts in the many-idead place of Joppa, a seaport town where cargo moves between the water and the land. The camels unload their cargo. Oh, Jerusalem, a day's journey over the hill, where the camels head with their cargo just arrived from the sea, passing through Joppa which is a border between— the houses and streets, the sun-caked marketplace. And God like a donkey to crate us to the sea.

I think of God clothed in the mast of the sea. I would ask what clothes God wears. I almost saw him once. Surely he has changes.

The waves embroider their little ridges on the shore. Sometimes I think the fish sew.

That night, the quarter moon is like the jagged edge of a broken tooth. I think of the crazy woman we buried; how we closed her mouth.

I am a crooked-toed old woman wrapped with my sewing. I would be nothing, but for Jesus. And my sewing.

The girl carries my basket for me to the marketplace. When she sees a puppet, she says nothing. I know she is thinking of Hannaput.

I see a sailor split open his leg on a nail. I could take my thread and needle and sew him up, if someone would hold him. The opening will ooze, and even the salt will not keep out death. It will enter him, has already, along the open shaft of his leg. I could bind the leg with cloth, but the cloth would sink into the wound.

Simon and the Christian men pray. *Euchontai* (they pray). *Euchai* (the prayers).

I do not think the sailor will survive. He will cross the water to heaven where I've been.

These are the ways of thinking, I tell the girl. It is what my grandmother taught me.

Dokein. To form an opinion, which can be either right or wrong. (Or considered both from different viewpoints.) *They think they will be heard because of their vain repetitions*? (Matthew 6:7).

Hegeisthai. To conclude. *I think myself happy*, said Paul the Apostle (Acts 26:2).

Noein. To perceive. Understand. Apprehend. *He can do more than we think* (Ephesians 3:20).

Huponoein. To surmise. *Who do you think I am?* Said John the Baptist (Acts 13:25).

Nomizein. To suppose. *Think not I am come to destroy the law. I am not come to destroy but to fulfill* (Matthew 5:17).

Logizrsthai. To reckon by calculation or imputation. *Whatever things are true, whatever things are honest, whatever things are just, whatever things are pure, whatever things are lovely, whatever things are of good report, if there be any virtue, and if there be any praise, think on these things* (Philippians 4:8).

Kataxiousthai. To count. *They were counted worthy to suffer shame for his name* (Acts 5:41).

Exouthenein. To make no account.

Oiesthai. To imagine. *I suppose that even the world itself could not contain the books that should be written* (John 21:25).

Phainein. To make an opinion. *What do you think?* (Mark 14:64).

Epiballein. To throw oneself upon. *And the second time the cock crowed. Peter called to mind the words that Jesus said to him. And when he thought of this, he wept* (Mark 14:72).

I repeat the ways of thinking to the girl. I think of other words for thought that my grandmother taught me. We live to think what we know, I tell the girl.

Phronein.

Axioun.

Enthumeisthai.

Huperphronein.

Dienthumeisthai.

The ways of thinking are nearly limitless.

"I still have not told you all," I tell her.

The girl falls at my feet as though dead. But she is acting.

I will give her to the traveling players, I say. She can be their puppet and ride over the desert on a camel. And sleep on the sand. And eat lizards which are tough as Simon's leather. Being in the sun.

I see that she is thinking. "You will dry like a fig. Your skin will darken." I see she looks at me. "Your eyes will yellow like mustard and saffron."

The girl holds her fingers in her ears.

I ask about the sailor when I am in the marketplace.

He is on a ship. They carried him on a litter, though I think it should be a bier.

Now the ship is ready to sail.

What would I tell him about dying if I had spoken? God clothes himself with words. Start memorizing scripture. I think you will need it there.

These are the ways of reasoning, I tell the girl. She seems at times to listen.

I mention her name in *ekklesia*. The men pray for her.

When I pray for her, I think of having patience.

Dialegesthai. To think different things with oneself.

Dialogizesthai. To bring together different reasons.

Sullogizesthai. To compute.

Suzetein. To examine. Discuss. Dispute.

The girl runs from the *ekklesia*.

In *ekklesia*, I request prayer for the girl again.

We hear that Paul whose name was Saul is in Ephesus.

I hear my needles call from the bottom of the sea as if they were the cargo ship that sank. Thoughts are bright needles that get us through this life. They are a fish-knife splitting the fish.

"Has Simon heard from Peter?" A woman asks as we sew at my house. Sometimes, they remember when he brought me back to life.

"He asked Jesus to bring me back to life," I correct them.

They look at me, but I don't have any words about death to tell them. Words have never been mine; they are strangers when I speak, a wind that should have brought a storm. If the words form in my mouth, my thoughts shut them down. It is better to be quiet. Maybe it's my thoughts that get in my way. I poke them with my needle to see if I am better without them also.

If only I had seen rolls of linen in heaven. If only I knew they were there. I could say I saw 100 spools of thread. 10 cases of needles. Ornaments of coral and pearls. I could say I saw parchments with drawings of cloaks and shawls and belts and tunics. The sun danced on them between the palm fronds, juggling its light. I want to know I can sew more tunics before they are turned into ephods. But there are not words for what I saw in heaven. Rolls of scrolls on the shelves. Fields, mountains and seas of people praising God. Creatures I have never seen. I cannot link. Sometimes my thoughts of heaven make me shudder.

I still can't eat figs. They remind me of leaches that swim in the water. If the women ask me again, I will say, I don't feel changed by death.

For all I know, I am still dead. Maybe there is no difference.

I think dying is slipping into heaven as if it were the sea. But the sea is a priest's ephod with its blue robe. There is a hole in the top of it, and a binding of woven work around the hole, as if a coat of mail, that it not rent. The priest's ephod and its robe are like the sea with a hole to fit the head into.

The sea is entering the moving garment of heaven, flowing on its journey, changing with thought, built upon what we know on earth of God, what we're aware of, what we think, how the thoughts form a relationship to God through Jesus. That's what

Jesus wants of us: our thoughts, which are jugglers. Maybe the purpose of life is to make the ephod we wear with him in heaven.

I sit in my house after the women are gone. What should I do now that I am back from death? Sometimes there is such loveliness in lighting the fire and cooking the barley cakes in olive oil. I do what I have to do here in my house. The ordinariness of it; the loveliness, loveliness. The camel trains and ships do not know I am here, yet I have been farther than they have. Maybe death is just another journey, getting up, walking through the door and out across the water under the firmament into heaven. If Christ be the place they want to go.

In *ekklesia*, I hear another scripture.

> *Ebedmelech took the men with him, and went into the house of the king, and took there old rags and worn-out garments, and let them down by cords into the dungeon to Jeremiah.*
>
> *And Ebedmelech, the Ethiopian, said unto Jeremiah, Put now these old rags and worn-out garments under your armpits under the cords. And Jeremiah did so.*
>
> *So they drew up Jeremiah with cords, and took him up out of the dungeon* (Jeremiah 38:11-13).

I could have told them that. It's clothes that pull us up.

Jesus, the resurrector of our cloth.

Even women could be priests like Samuel and Aaron. Hadn't I thought so in heaven? Hadn't I seen the holy garments? The closets of coats, the robes of the ephod, the ephods, the breast-plates, girdles, and the mitres which are the thoughts embroidered in the head. Weren't they for all? Women the same as men.

In the end, if they keep bothering me, I will tell them, it is the self alone that survives.

In the end, I will tell them, it's what we sew.

Afterword

I wanted to write about Dorcas because her voice kept returning to my imagination. Not much is said about her in the New Testament.

She lived in the first century after Christ.

She sewed in Joppa on the Mediterranean, some thirty-five miles from Jerusalem.

She died.

She was brought back to life by the Apostle, Peter.

I wanted to explore her life through writing. I wanted to know the possibilities, even if a gist, or a *somewhere-in-the-neighborhood-of*.

I began by questioning. What was her life like? What happened when she died? When she returned to life? What can be known of history anyway?

Thinking in terms of the desert region where she lived, I wanted a mirage of her life, with imagination as *fill-in* between fragments of the Old and New Testaments. I wanted to hear her voice before the event of her death. I wanted to hear it after she returned to her life.

Dorcas was full of good works, yet there had to be frailties of the human sort. I wanted to see her sewing and sewing, making garments and garments. I wanted to see her clothed with the New Testament life.

I would like to thank Bruce Eldevick at the Northwestern Lutheran Seminary, Minneapolis, for guiding me to some books on New Testament life. A *Dictionary of Life in Bible Times*, edited by Edouard Urech, Oxford University Press, 1960, was one of them.

Also, Ruth Dolman at Northwestern College, St. Paul.

Also, *Vine's Expository Dictionary of New Testament Words*, edited by W.E. Vine, Riverside Book and Bible House, Iowa Falls, Iowa.

I thank also Revelation 22:18-19, which says,

> *If any man shall add unto these things, God shall add unto him the plagues that are written in this book;*
>
> *And if any man shall take away from the words of the book of this prophecy, God shall take away his part out of the book of life, and out of the holy city, and from the things which are written in this book.*

I thought about that severe admonition as I wrote.

But I wanted to continue writing about Dorcas.

I wanted to fill-in the blank places in the scriptures, even if they were only the imaginary happenings of Dorcas' ordinary daily life.

I wanted to work with the process of writing about someone who lived, whose life and words are not known. I wanted Dorcas to speak, even if it had to be in a language not her own.

Maybe she wasn't familiar with all the happenings in the New Testament, as I have her in the book. But I wanted to take her character and have her buried woman's voice speak away the mantle put on it by time and custom.

I wanted the thoughts of Dorcas to speak. I wanted to hear what she was thinking.

I wanted her transfigured voice. I wanted to sew her story.

I also wanted to work through my own sense of personal transgression, which I felt while writing.

I had the feeling of being where I didn't belong, which all writing is, maybe, even when it isn't putting words into the mouth of someone who lived. Someone who probably would not want those words there.

But I wanted to write about Dorcas as a woman who had a heart for others, who was full of good works and charitable deeds. I wanted to hear her talk about the tunics and garments she made, day after day, and why she made them.

But I couldn't get to the voice that would say it. I only got those short declarative sentences. She may have retained her privacy and silence after all. And this story is a garment, and not the person beneath it. In spite of her kindness and benevolence, she may have kept her own fierce way of not giving of herself.

In the end, this story may not even be a garment, but loose threads knotted around this unknown character that can be picked off.

Lastly, thanks to David Hopper, James Wallace Professor in Religious Studies at Macalester College for our conversation, and to Connie Brouillette for her careful reading of the manuscript. Thanks also to Jeremiah Reedy, Professor of Classics at Macalester College for help with the Greek.

Grace and peace be multiplied.

Other Books by Diane Glancy

Novels

Pushing the Bear

The Only Piece of Furniture in the House

Flutie

Fuller Man

Stories

Trigger Dance

Firesticks

Monkey Secret

The Voice That Was in Travel

Essays

Claiming Breath

The West Pole

The Cold-and-Hunger Dance

Plays

War Cries

Poems

Offering

One Age in a Dream

Lone Dog's Winter Count

Iron Woman

Boom Town

Coyote's Quodlibet

Primer of the Obsolete

(Ado)ration

Anthologies

Braided Lives

Two Worlds Walking

Visit Teepee Town: Native Writings after the Detours

DIANE GLANCY is Associate Professor at Macalester College in St. Paul where she teaches Native American Literature and Creative Writing. She has received a National Endowment for the Arts, a National Endowment for the Humanities, a Minnesota Book Award and a National Book Award. She received her M.F.A. from the University of Iowa.

Two books of poetry by Diane Glancy, A *Primer for the Obsolete*, and *(Ado)ration*, have also been published by Chax Press.